THE LIZARD'S TAIL

KARADI TALES

Shobha Viswanath
Christine Kastl

A baby lizard hopped from one place to
another and scooted through open drawers
and shelves.

Tanya pushed her drawer shut.
'Chop-slice,' went the lizard's tail.

'Have you have lost your tail?'
asked the lizard's mother, smiling.
'Perhaps, it's time for a new look!'

A new look? What did she mean?

As he thought about this, he
saw a squirrel running up and
down the chickoo tree.
Swishing her bushy tail, the
squirrel asked, 'Hey, little
lizard, what's up with you?'

'I seem to have lost my tail.
I really like yours.
Can I have it?'

'I am sorry,' she said. 'I can't give my
tail. I use it for shade in the summer
and warmth in the winter.
Also, when these silly monkeys push
me off my tree, if I didn't have my tail,
I could get hurt.'

Across the street was the milkman's cow. Long and thin, like a whip, the cow's tail was fascinating.

'Mrs. Cow, Mrs. Cow!' the lizard called out. 'Do you have an extra tail?'

'Wish I did!' mooed Mrs. Cow. 'I could do with an extra one to keep these nasty flies off my back!'

'Oh dear,' thought the lizard. 'Isn't there anyone who will give me a tail?'

Horn Please

He saw three dogs at the street corner
and darted towards them. 'Hello there,
I have lost my tail. Would one of you be
able to spare your curly ones?'

The largest of the dogs began to laugh and the
rest joined him. There was a howl of laughter.
Their tails wagged merrily.

Disappointed, the lizard moved on.

Nearby on a wall, an orange cat yawned
gracefully and purred, 'My tail keeps me
balanced when I climb fences. What would
I do without it?'

At the temple gate an elephant
saw the lizard approaching out
of the corner of his eye and said,
'Can I help you, little one?'

'No one has been able to help me
and all I want is a tail!'

The elephant laughed, 'I know you have lost your tail, but just imagine yourself with a cow's tail or a squirrel's! How will you dart across the ceiling with a dog's tail or a cat's? You would look ridiculous!'

The lizard tried to imagine himself with a cow's tail. 'Yes, I would look silly!' he laughed.

He thanked the elephant, ran home and
told his mother the whole story.

'You silly thing! Just turn around,' she said.
The little lizard saw that his tail was no
longer a stump. It had started to grow.
Delighted, he let out a squeal.

Scqueee!

Soon, the tail was fully grown. He was
wearing a new look. It was perfect!

The Lizard's Tail

Second Reprint 2013

Text: Shobha Viswanath
Illustrations: Christine Kastl

Karadi Tales Company Pvt. Ltd.
3A Dev Regency 11 First Main Road Gandhinagar Adyar Chennai 600020
Ph: +91 44 4205 4243 Email: contact@karaditales.com
Website: www.karaditales.com

Distributed in North America by Consortium Book Sales & Distribution
The Keg House 34 Thirteenth Avenue NE Suite 101 Minneapolis MN 55413-1006 USA
Orders: (+1) 731-423-1550 orderentry@perseusbooks.com
Electronic ordering via PUBNET (SAN 631760X) Website: www.cbsd.com

Printed in India
ISBN 978-81-8190-150-7